The Painter's Three Wishes

Jibber Jabber

ACKNOWLEDGEMENTS

Illustrator: Quynh Rua

Editor: Jessie Raymond

Proofreaders: Gwen Peterson, Jenny Dulaney

Special thanks to the Mitchell family.

Once upon a time, in a kingdom far away, there lived an old woman. The woman was kind, but like most kind people in fairy tales, she was poor. However, she still worked hard and saved what little money she could earn. At the end of every month, if she had enough coins, she bought herself a treat: a small bowl of delicious chocolate pudding.

This woman had a son. When he worked, he was a painter, but he seldom worked for he was lazy and selfish. He did not live with his mother. He would only visit once a month – at the end of the month when his mother had the chocolate pudding. The painter would come and ask for some of the dessert. His mother would let him eat most of it, leaving only a little for herself. After eating, the painter would spend the night at his mother's house, sleeping in the only bed, while his mother slept in a hammock. The next day when he left, he would ask his mother for money. His mother would give him some, leaving only a few coins for herself. He would leave, only coming back at the end of the month to do it all over again.

But one day, something changed. At the end of the month, as the old woman was walking home with the chocolate pudding she bought, she saw a beggar. The people in town were usually nice, but they all avoided this beggar because she looked strange. The beggar had four eyes, two mouths, and no nose. When the old woman saw that no one would help the beggar, she invited her to stay in her home. As soon as her son saw the strange guest, he told his mother to throw her out. All four of the beggar's eyes began to fill with tears. His mother insisted that the stranger would stay. This upset the painter, but since it was not his home, he could do nothing about it. All he could do was complain, which he did, and loudly so.

The three of them ate supper. The whole time, the painter ridiculed the beggar and bragged about how important he was. He was going to paint a portrait of a duchess. Soon, his work would be so admired, that kings and queens would ask him to paint their portraits as well. After supper, when the time came to eat the chocolate pudding, the painter took most of it. The old woman gave the beggar what was left, and had none to eat. When it was time to sleep, the painter slept on the bed, the beggar slept in the hammock, and the old woman slept on the floor. The next morning, the mother gave her son some money and gave the beggar what few coins she had left.

While the painter still stood there complaining, a blue light started to glow around the beggar. She was transformed into a beautiful fairy with four wings and two antennas, but still no nose.

The fairy fluttered to the old woman and said, "I have come to help you, kind woman. I will return your three acts of kindness for three wishes. You have given me food, a place to sleep, and money. I will grant you better food, a better home, and more money."

"Thank you, kind fairy," the old woman said, "but it is not I who needs your help. If you could help my son, that would make me happiest in all the world."

"Are you sure you want to give your gifts to this person?" asked the fairy.

"Yes, of course."

"Very well. I don't think that's wise, but you may use your gifts in any way you like." The fairy turned to the painter and asked him, "Which wish would you like first: food, a home, or money?"

The painter said he would take the food first. He complained that he was still hungry after the small breakfast his mother gave him. The fairy handed the painter a seed.

"Take this seed and plant it in the yard. For seven days, you must water the ground and pull out all the weeds. If you do this, a tree will grow. This tree will grow both red apples and golden pears. One red apple is all it takes for someone who is hungry to be satisfied for a whole week. However, no one must eat the golden pears. Whoever takes one bite of the pear, will instantly have the face of an animal, and the entire tree will shrivel up and never grow fruit again."

After the fairy promised to return when she was needed, she disappeared in a cloud of blue confetti. The lazy painter had no intention of caring for a tree. He handed the seed to his mother and left. His mother planted the seed, and for seven days she watered it and pulled out any weeds.

After the seven days, she walked out into her yard and saw an enchanted tree with red apples and golden pears. Whenever the old woman was hungry, she ate an apple, and was satisfied for an entire week. The old woman also gave some apples to her neighbors, but she was careful never to eat or give away the pears.

At the end of the month, the old woman bought a small bowl of chocolate pudding. The painter came home as usual. As the painter and his mother ate an apple each for supper, he complained that the duchess refused to buy his portrait of her. She had criticized his work, calling it mediocre, after he had spent nearly two hours painting it.

After supper, the painter ate most of the chocolate pudding, leaving only a little for his mother. While they ate, his mother told him that the magical apples worked. She and her neighbors would never have to go hungry again. The painter did nothing but complain. She shouldn't share the apples, he said, for it was his tree and not hers.

At night, the mother slept soundly in the hammock, but the painter could not sleep, even though he was lying on a comfortable bed. He was still angry at the duchess. He stayed up, tossing and turning in bed, until he thought of a plan. He chuckled at his clever idea and drifted off to sleep.

The next morning, after his mother gave him money, he sneaked into the yard and picked a pear from the tree. He strolled to the duchess' castle. He told her he had a present for her, to apologize for his mediocre work. The duchess said she did not want a present, but the painter insisted. He handed her the golden pear. As soon as the duchess took a bite, the tree that grew the apples and pears shriveled up, and the duchess' face became like the face of a walrus.

The duchess was horrified. Having the face of a walrus would be fine if she was married, but she had no husband yet. Who would marry her now? The painter then suggested it would be a good idea for her to buy his portrait. She could use it to trick any suitors. The duchess did not know what else to do. She was too scared to have her portrait painted by another painter. She didn't want anyone else to see her, because word might get out that she had the face of a walrus. So, the duchess bought the portrait, at five times the original price, and sent it to the Prince of the Ivory Castle. The prince saw her portrait, thought she was beautiful, and agreed to get married without even meeting her. Imagine his surprise at the wedding, when he lifted the veil, and discovered he was married to a woman with a walrus-face.

The prince was angry at the terrible trick. He was so mad, he sent guards after the painter. The guards brought him to the Ivory Castle to stand before the prince and his walrus-faced wife. The prince ordered the painter to be imprisoned for the rest of his life. The painter was locked in a room at the top of an ivory tower. It took one thousand steps to go up and two thousand steps to go down. There was no way the painter could ever escape, or so he thought.

Although the painter was in prison, the prince allowed his mother to visit. It was the end of the month, so she brought a small bowl of chocolate pudding. She huffed and panted up the thousand steps and at last reached her son. Her son ate most of the pudding, leaving only a little for his mother. His mother was distraught that her son would be locked up for the rest of his life. The painter was upset as well and made sure to complain loudly.

"I can't spend the rest of my life in this ivory tower! This isn't a home! I demand a better place to stay!"

Suddenly, there was a cloud of blue confetti, and the fairy appeared.

"Would you like to use another wish?" asked the fairy. "Would you like to wish for a better home?"

"Yes! If it will get me out of here!" The painter said.

The fairy gave the painter a spinning wheel and said, "You must spin this spinning wheel for seven days. After seven days, you will make a magic flying carpet. The carpet will ask if you want to go to a house made of stone or to a house made of diamonds. You must say, 'Take me to the house of stone.' Do not be greedy and ask for the house of diamonds. Ask for the house of stone, and that house will be yours. You will live a comfortable life in a comfortable home."

Then the fairy disappeared in a cloud of blue confetti. The painter refused to work the spinning wheel. The old woman wanted her son out of prison, so she carried the spinning wheel with her, huffing and panting down the two thousand steps. For seven days, she spun the wheel, and made a magic flying carpet. By the eighth day, she carried it up the thousand steps of the ivory tower to her son, for he had forbidden her to fly on it. He should be the first to use it; it was his gift after all.

"Do you want to go to the house made of stone, or the house made of diamonds?" The carpet asked the painter.

The painter was greedy of course and answered, "Take me to the house of diamonds!"

He jumped on the carpet and flew away, leaving his mother to walk down the two thousand steps and return to her own humble cottage. The carpet took the painter to a home made entirely of diamonds. After dropping him off at the diamond door, the carpet flew away. The house was huge! In fact, everything was huge! Inside the house, there was a huge table made of diamonds, a huge chair made of diamonds, even a huge jewelry box made of diamonds which contained even more diamonds! The painter spent the night in the huge bed of diamonds, which was surprisingly comfortable, and drifted off to sleep.

The next morning, he was woken by an angry giant. This diamond home belonged to the giant, and she was angry someone had come in and slept in her diamond bed. She threw the painter out and slammed the large diamond door. The painter called for the magic carpet, but it would not come back, so he started to make his way back to his mother's house. By the time he reached her, it was the end of the month. The painter ate most of her chocolate pudding, leaving only a little for his mother.

Fortunately, the painter found some work. The king said he would pay him to paint portraits of his two daughters. The older daughter was 22, while the younger was 21. They should have been married years ago and were far too old to still be unwed, but the king had been too busy to marry them off. So, he decided lovely portraits would help attract potential suitors.

The painter began his work, which was both easy and difficult depending on which daughter he was painting. The older daughter was arrogant, rude, and condescending. She called the painter names and made fun of him for being poor. She was rich, would marry someone rich, would have rich children and a rich cat, and live a rich life; while he was poor and no one would ever want to marry him.

The younger daughter was kind to the painter, for she treated everyone with kindness. One day, while he was painting the younger princess' portrait, her heart seemed to beat a little faster and also skip a beat at the same time. Her heart felt heavy but her body felt light as a feather. She felt sick to her stomach but it also seemed to be filled with butterflies. Because she certainly was not ill, this could only mean one thing: She realized that she must be in love with the painter. She told him this, and the painter, seeing her beauty and her wealth, told her that he was in love with her too and promised to marry her. The princess was thrilled! She asked her father if she could marry the painter. The king said she could marry whomever she liked as long as her suitor was rich and could gift the king a large sum of money.

Of course, the painter was not rich, so after he finished their portraits, he was paid his fee and sent away. Once the painter spent his money, which did not take long, he returned to his mother. It was the end of the month again, so the painter ate most of the chocolate pudding as usual, leaving only a little for his mother. He said he needed money to marry a princess. His mother offered everything she had, but it would not be enough.

The painter noticed a cloud of blue confetti. The fairy appeared again and asked if the painter would like to use his third wish, the wish for money. The painter was more than happy to use his third wish, so the fairy gave him a large bag. He opened the large bag and a clucking chicken leaped out, nearly pecking off his nose.

"You must feed the chicken and fluff its feathers every day for seven days. Then, whenever you want money, tell the chicken to lay an egg," the fairy instructed.

"All I get is an egg?" whined the painter.

"Not just any egg, a golden egg. The chicken will lay as many golden eggs as you wish, but on one condition: You must use your money to marry the younger princess. If you break your promise to her and marry another, the chicken will no longer lay golden eggs, and all of the gold it has made will turn to dust."

As you can probably guess, the painter was not going to take care of a chicken He left that for his mother to do. Each day, his mother fed the chicken and fluffed its feathers. After the seven days, the painter returned. The chicken was laying golden eggs. The painter ordered the chicken to keep laying eggs, until the whole cottage was filled with them.

The painter went to the king. He now had enough money to marry a princess. The king called his two daughters and asked the painter which one he wanted to marry. The younger daughter was so happy to see him. The older daughter was happy too. She was much friendlier now that he was rich. The older daughter said she would be delighted to marry him.

The painter, happy to have two choices now instead of only one, said he needed a day to think about it. He went home, and his mother begged him to marry the younger daughter or else they would lose all the gold. The painter thought that was a wise decision, but he would not admit it. He did not like being told what to do. He was upset the fairy always gave him two choices when in reality there was always only one. That night, as he was lying in his mother's comfortable bed, he devised what he thought was a clever idea. If he chose the older daughter, all of his gold would disappear, but he would still be married to a princess. The king was rich and would provide them with money and any other luxuries they would want. Besides, the older one was prettier.

The painter decided to marry the older daughter. The younger sister was heartbroken. The painter gave the king a chest filled with golden eggs as payment for the dowry. The next week, the painter married the older princess, and the younger princess was married to someone else, someone not as rich but also not as selfish as the painter. The day after the wedding, the king opened the chest of golden eggs only to discover that all the gold had turned to dust. Likewise, all gold that the painter had was turned to dust.

The older daughter cried. Though she knew her father would provide for them, she felt as if she was living in poverty compared to the wealth she could have had. It was her worst nightmare: Now she was poor and would have poor children and a poor cat and live a poor life. When the painter laughed and mocked her, her misery turned into anger. She ran back to her father and demanded revenge on the painter. The king issued a decree which welcomed anyone to challenge the painter to a duel for humiliating the princess. If the painter refused to fight, he would immediately be put to death.

Everyone heard the proclamation, including the Prince of the Ivory Castle. He had not forgotten the painter and was determined that he would not escape punishment this time. He eagerly challenged the painter to a duel, and the painter had no choice but to accept. Early in the morning, they crossed swords and fought. The prince lunged and drove his sword into the painter's heart, killing him instantly. The older princess was satisfied. She then began her search for another husband, and the Prince of the Ivory Castle returned home to his walrus-faced wife.

The painter's mother was sad, for she had loved her son dearly. However, she was happy about one thing. At the end of the month, when she bought her chocolate pudding, she was able to eat the whole thing all by herself.

The End

https://jibberjabberblog.blogspot.com/2023/11/video-tp3w.html

You can download free bookmarks here!

https://jibberjabberblog.blogspot.com/2023/11/extras-tp3w.html